Praise for Brandon Sanderson:

'Anyone looking for a different and refreshing fantasy novel will be delighted by this exceptional tale'
Michael Moorcock on *Warbreaker*

'Highly recommended to anyone hungry for a good read'
Robin Hobb on *The Final Empire*

'Brandon Sanderson is the real thing – an exciting storyteller with a unique and powerful vision'
David Farland

'Sanderson will be forever mentioned as one of the finest fantasy writers of this generation'
Fantasy Faction

'Sanderson is clearly a master of large-scale stories, splendidly depicting worlds as well as strong female characters'
Booklist

Also by Brandon Sanderson from Gollancz:

LEGION

BRANDON SANDERSON

GOLLANCZ

LONDON

Copyright © Dragonsteel Entertainment, LLC 2012
All rights reserved

The right of Brandon Sanderson to be identified as the author
of this work has been asserted by him in accordance with the
Copyright, Designs and Patents Act 1988.

First published in Great Britain in 2013 by Gollancz
An imprint of the Orion Publishing Group
Carmelite House, 50 Victoria Embankment,
London EC4Y 0DZ

An Hachette UK Company

This edition published in Great Britain in 2015
by Gollancz

A CIP catalogue record for this book
is available from the British Library

ISBN 978 1 473 21263 3

1 3 5 7 9 10 8 6 4 2

Typeset by Input Data Services Ltd, Bridgwater, Somerset

Printed in Great Britain by Clays Ltd, St Ives plc

The Orion Publishing Group's policy is to use papers that
are natural, renewable and recyclable products and made
from wood grown in sustainable forests. The logging and
manufacturing processes are expected to conform to the
environmental regulations of the country of origin.

www.brandonsanderson.com
www.orionbooks.co.uk
www.gollancz.co.uk

For Daniel Wells, who gave me the idea.

MY NAME IS Stephen Leeds, and I am perfectly sane. My hallucinations, however, are all quite mad.

The gunshots coming from J.C.'s room popped like firecrackers. Grumbling to myself, I grabbed the earmuffs hanging outside his door – I'd learned to keep them there – and pushed my way in. J.C. wore his own earmuffs, his handgun raised in two hands, sighting at a picture of Osama bin Laden on the wall.

Beethoven was playing. Very loudly.

'I was trying to have a conversation!' I yelled.

J.C. didn't hear me. He emptied a clip into bin Laden's face, punching an assortment of holes through the wall in the process. I didn't dare get close. He might accidentally shoot me if I surprised him.

I didn't know what would happen if one of my hallucinations shot me. How would my mind interpret that? Undoubtedly, there were a dozen psychologists who'd want to write a paper on it. I wasn't inclined to give them the opportunity.

'J.C.!' I screamed as he stopped to reload.

He glanced toward me, then grinned, taking off his earmuffs. Any grin from J.C. looks half like a scowl, but I'd long ago learned to stop being intimidated by him.

'Eh, skinny,' he said, holding up the handgun. 'Care to fire off a clip or two? You could use the practice.'

I took the gun from him. 'We had a shooting range installed in the mansion for a purpose, J.C. *Use it.*'

'Terrorists don't usually find me in a shooting range. Well, it did happen that once. Pure coincidence.'

I sighed, taking the remote from the end table, then turning down the music. J.C. reached out, pointing the tip of the gun up in the air, then moving my finger off the trigger. 'Safety first, kid.'

'It's an imaginary gun anyway,' I said, handing it back to him.

'Yeah, sure.'

J.C. doesn't believe that he's a hallucination, which is unusual. Most of them accept it, to one extent or another. Not J.C. Big without being bulky, square-faced but not distinctive, he had the eyes of a killer. Or so he claimed. Perhaps he kept them in his pocket.

He slapped a new clip into the gun, then eyed the picture of bin Laden.

'Don't,' I warned.

'But—'

'He's dead anyway. They got him ages ago.'

'That's a story we told the public, skinny.' J.C. holstered the gun. 'I'd explain, but you don't have clearance.'

'Stephen?' a voice came from the doorway.

I turned. Tobias is another hallucination – or 'aspect,' as I sometimes call them. Lanky and ebony-skinned, he had dark freckles on his age-wrinkled cheeks. He kept his greying hair very short, and wore a loose, informal business suit with no necktie.

'I was merely wondering,' Tobias said, 'how long you intend to keep that poor man waiting.'

'Until he leaves,' I said, joining Tobias in the hallway. The two of us began walking away from J.C.'s room.

'He was very polite, Stephen,' Tobias said.

Behind us, J.C. started shooting again. I groaned.

'I'll go speak to J.C.,' Tobias said in a soothing voice. 'He's just trying to keep up his skills. He wants to be of use to you.'

'Fine, whatever.' I left Tobias and rounded a corner in the lush mansion. I had forty-seven rooms. They were nearly all filled. At the end of the hallway, I entered a small room decorated with a Persian rug and wood panels. I threw myself down on the black leather couch in the center.

Ivy sat at her chair beside the couch. 'You intend to continue through *that*?' she asked over the sound of the gunshots.

'Tobias is going to speak to him.'

'I see,' Ivy said, making a notation on her notepad. She wore a dark business suit, with slacks and a jacket. Her blonde hair was up in a bun. She was in her early forties, and was one of the aspects I'd had the longest.

'How does it make you feel,' she said, 'that your projections are beginning to disobey you?'

'Most do obey me,' I said defensively. 'J.C. has *never* paid attention to what I tell him. That hasn't changed.'

'You deny that it's getting worse?'

I didn't say anything.

She made a notation.

'You turned away another petitioner, didn't you?' Ivy asked. 'They come to you for help.'

'I'm busy.'

'Doing what? Listening to gunshots? Going more mad?'

'I'm *not* going more mad,' I said. 'I've stabilized. I'm practically normal. Even my non-hallucinatory psychiatrist acknowledges that.'

Ivy said nothing. In the distance, the gunshots finally stopped, and I sighed in relief, raising my fingers to my temples. 'The formal definition of insanity,' I said, 'is actually quite fluid. Two people can have the exact same condition, with the exact same severity, but one can be considered *sane* by the official standards while the other is considered *insane*. You cross the line into insanity when your mental state stops you from being able to function, from being able to have a normal life. By those standards, I'm not the least bit insane.'

'You call this a normal life?' she asked.

'It works well enough.' I glanced to the side. Ivy had covered up the wastebasket with a clipboard, as usual.

Tobias entered a few moments later. 'That petitioner is still there, Stephen.'

'What?' Ivy said, giving me a glare. 'You're making the poor man wait? It's been *four hours*.'

'All right, fine!' I leaped off the couch. 'I'll send him away.' I strode out of the room and down the steps to the ground floor, into the grand entryway.

Wilson, my butler – who is a real person, not a hallucination – stood outside the closed door to the sitting room. He looked over his bifocals at me.

'You too?' I asked.

'Four hours, master?'

'I had to get myself under control, Wilson.'

'You like to use that excuse, Master Leeds. One wonders if moments like this are a matter of laziness more than control.'

'You're not paid to wonder things like that,' I said.

4

He raised an eyebrow, and I felt ashamed. Wilson didn't deserve snappishness; he was an excellent servant, and an excellent person. It wasn't easy to find house staff willing to put up with my ... particularities.

'I'm sorry,' I said. 'I've been feeling a little worn down lately.'

'I will fetch you some lemonade, Master Leeds,' he said. 'For ...'

'Three of us,' I said, nodding to Tobias and Ivy – who, of course, Wilson couldn't see. 'Plus the petitioner.'

'No ice in mine, please,' Tobias said.

'I'll have a glass of water instead,' Ivy added.

'No ice for Tobias,' I said, absently pushing open the door. 'Water for Ivy.'

Wilson nodded, off to do as requested. He *was* a good butler. Without him, I think I'd go insane.

A young man in a polo shirt and slacks waited in the sitting room. He leaped up from one of the chairs. 'Master Legion?'

I winced at the nickname. That had been chosen by a particularly gifted psychologist. Gifted in dramatics, that is. Not really so much in the psychology department.

'Call me Stephen,' I said, holding the door for Ivy and Tobias. 'What can we do for you?'

'We?' the boy asked.

'Figure of speech,' I said, walking into the room and taking one of the chairs across from the young man.

'I ... uh ... I hear you help people, when nobody else will.' The boy swallowed. 'I brought two thousand. Cash.' He tossed an envelope with my name and address on it onto the table.

'That'll buy you a consultation,' I said, opening it and doing a quick count.

Tobias gave me a look. He hates it when I charge people,

but you don't get a mansion with enough rooms to hold all your hallucinations by working for free. Besides, judging from his clothing, this kid could afford it.

'What's the problem?' I asked.

'My fiancée,' the young man said, taking something out of his pocket. 'She's been cheating on me.'

'My condolences,' I said. 'But we're *not* private investigators. We don't do surveillance.'

Ivy walked through the room, not sitting down. She strolled around the young man's chair, inspecting him.

'I know,' the boy said quickly. 'I just … well, she's vanished, you see.'

Tobias perked up. He likes a good mystery.

'He's not telling us everything,' Ivy said, arms folded, one finger tapping her other arm.

'You sure?' I asked.

'Oh, yes,' the boy said, assuming I'd spoken to him. 'She's gone, though she did leave this note.' He unfolded it and set it on the table. 'The really strange thing is, I think there might be some kind of cipher to it. Look at these words. They don't make sense.'

I picked up the paper, scanning the words he indicated. They were on the back of the sheet, scrawled quickly, like a list of notes. The same paper had later been used as a farewell letter from the fiancée. I showed it to Tobias.

'That's Plato,' he said, pointing to the notes on the back. 'Each is a quote from the *Phaedrus*. Ah, Plato. Remarkable man, you know. Few people are aware that he was actually a *slave* at one point, sold on the market by a tyrant who disagreed with his politics – that and the turning of the tyrant's brother into a disciple. Fortunately, Plato was purchased by someone familiar with his work, an admirer you might say, who freed him. It does pay to have loving fans, even in ancient Greece ...'

Tobias continued on. He had a deep, comforting voice, which I liked to listen to. I examined the note, then looked up at Ivy, who shrugged.

The door opened, and Wilson entered with the lemonade and Ivy's water. I noticed J.C. standing outside, his gun out as he peeked into the room and inspected the young man. J.C.'s eyes narrowed.

'Wilson,' I said, taking my lemonade, 'would you kindly send for Audrey?'

'Certainly, master,' the butler said. I knew, somewhere deep within, that he had not *really* brought cups for Ivy and Tobias, though he made an act of handing something to the empty chairs. My mind filled in the rest, imagining drinks, imagining Ivy strolling over to pluck hers from Wilson's hand as he tried to give it to where he thought she was sitting. She smiled at him fondly.

Wilson left.

'Well?' the young man asked. 'Can you—'

He cut off as I held up a finger. Wilson couldn't see my projections, but he knew their rooms. We had to hope that Audrey was in. She had a habit of visiting her sister in Springfield.

Fortunately, she walked into the room a few minutes later. She was, however, wearing a bathrobe. 'I assume this is important,' she said, drying her hair with a towel.

I held up the note, then the envelope with the money. Audrey leaned down. She was a dark-haired woman, a little on the chunky side. She'd joined us a few years back, when I'd been working on a counterfeiting case.

She mumbled to herself for a minute or two, taking out a magnifying glass – I was amused that she kept one in her bathrobe, but that was Audrey for you – and looking from the note to the envelope and back. One had supposedly been written by the fiancée, the other by the young man.

Audrey nodded. 'Definitely the same hand.'

'It's not a very big sample,' I said.

'It's what?' the boy asked.

'It's enough in this case,' Audrey said. 'The envelope has your full name and address. Line slant, word spacing, letter formation … all give the same answer. He also has a very distinctive *e*. If we use the longer sample as the exemplar, the envelope sample can be determined as authentic – in my estimation – at over a ninety percent reliability.'

'Thanks,' I said.

'I could use a new dog,' she said, strolling away.

'I'm *not* imagining you a puppy, Audrey. J.C. creates enough racket! I don't want a dog running around here barking.'

'Oh, come on,' she said, turning at the doorway. 'I'll feed it fake food and give it fake water and take it on fake walks. Everything a fake puppy could want.'

'Out with you,' I said, though I was smiling. She was teasing. It was nice to have some aspects who didn't mind being hallucinations. The young man regarded me with a baffled expression.

'You can drop the act,' I said to him.

'Act?'

'The act that you're surprised by how "strange" I am. This was a fairly amateur attempt. You're a grad student, I assume?'

He got a panicked look in his eyes.

'Next time, have a roommate write the note for you,' I said, tossing it back to him. 'Damn it, I don't have time for this.' I stood up.

'You could give him an interview,' Tobias said.

'After he lied to me?' I snapped.

'Please,' the boy said, standing. 'My girlfriend …'

'You called her a fiancée before,' I said, turning. 'You're here to try to get me to take on a "case," during which you will lead me around by the nose while you secretly take notes about my condition. Your real purpose is to write a dissertation or something.'

His face fell. Ivy stood behind him, shaking her head in disdain.

'You think you're the first one to think of this?' I asked.

He grimaced. 'You can't blame a guy for trying.'

'I can and I do,' I said. 'Often. Wilson! We're going to need security!'

'No need,' the boy said, grabbing his things. In his haste, a miniature recorder slipped out of his shirt pocket and rattled against the table.

I raised an eyebrow as he blushed, snatched the recorder, then dashed from the room.

Tobias rose and walked over to me, his hands clasped behind his back. 'Poor lad. And he'll probably have to walk home, too. In the rain.'

'It's raining?'

'Stan says it will come soon,' Tobias said. 'Have you considered that they would try things like this less often if you would agree to an interview now and then?'

'I'm tired of being referenced in case studies,' I said, waving a hand in annoyance. 'I'm tired of being poked and prodded. I'm tired of being special.'

'What?' Ivy said, amused. 'You'd rather work a day job at a desk? Give up the spacious mansion?'

'I'm not saying there aren't perks,' I said as Wilson walked back in, turning his head to watch the youth flee out the front door. 'Make sure he actually goes, would you please, Wilson?'

'Of course, master.' He handed me a tray with the day's mail on it, then left.

I looked through the mail. He'd already removed the bills and the junk mail. That left a letter from my human psychologist, which I ignored, and a nondescript white envelope, large sized.

I frowned, taking it and ripping open the top. I took out the contents.

There was only one thing in the envelope. A single photograph, five by eight, in black and white. I raised an eyebrow. It was a picture of a rocky coast where a couple of small trees clung to a rock extending out into the ocean.

'Nothing on the back,' I said as Tobias and Ivy looked over my shoulder. 'Nothing else in the envelope.'

'It's from someone else trying to fish for an interview, I'll bet,' Ivy said. 'They're doing a better job than the kid.'

'It doesn't look like anything special,' J.C. said, shoving his way up beside Ivy, who punched him in the shoulder. 'Rocks. Trees. Boring.'

'I don't know . . .' I said. 'There's something about it. Tobias?'

Tobias took the photograph. At least, that's what I saw. Most likely I still had the photo in my hand, but I couldn't feel it there, now that I perceived Tobias holding it. It's strange, the way the mind can change perception.

Tobias studied the picture for a long moment. J.C. began clicking his pistol's safety off and on.

'Aren't you always talking about gun safety?' Ivy hissed at him.

'I'm being safe,' he said. 'Barrel's not pointed at anyone. Besides, I have keen, iron control over every muscle in my body. I could—'

'Hush, both of you,' Tobias said. He held the picture closer. 'My God ...'

'Please don't use the Lord's name in vain,' Ivy said.

J.C. snorted.

'Stephen,' Tobias said. 'Computer.'

I joined him at the sitting room's desktop, then sat down, Tobias leaning over my shoulder. 'Do a search for the Lone Cypress.'

I did so, and brought up image view. A couple dozen shots of the same rock appeared on the screen, but all of them had a larger tree growing on it. The tree in these photos was fully grown; in fact, it looked ancient.

'Okay, great,' J.C. said. 'Still trees. Still rocks. Still boring.'

'That's the Lone Cypress, J.C.,' Tobias said. 'It's famous, and is believed to be *at least* two hundred and fifty years old.'

'So ... ?' Ivy asked.

I held up the photograph that had been mailed. 'In this, it's no more than ... what? Ten?'

'Likely younger,' Tobias said.

'So for this to be real,' I said, 'it would have to have been taken in the mid to late 1700s. Decades before the camera was invented.'

'LOOK, IT'S OBVIOUSLY a fake,' Ivy said. 'I don't see why you two are so bothered by this.'

Tobias and I strolled the hallway of the mansion. It had been two days. I still couldn't get the image out of my head. I carried the photo in my jacket pocket.

'A hoax *would* be the most rational explanation, Stephen,' Tobias said.

'Armando thinks it's real,' I said.

'Armando is a complete loon,' Ivy replied. Today she wore a grey business suit.

'True,' I said, then raised a hand to my pocket again. Altering the photo wouldn't have taken much. What was doctoring a photo, these days? Practically any kid with Photoshop could create realistic fakes.

Armando had run it through some advanced programs, checking levels and doing a bunch of other things that were too technical for me to understand, but he admitted that didn't mean anything. A talented artist could fool the tests.

So why did this photo haunt me so?

'This smacks of someone trying to prove something,' I said. 'There are many trees older than the Lone Cypress, but few are in as distinctive a location. This photograph is intended to be instantly recognizable as impossible, at least to those with a good knowledge of history.'

'All the more likely a hoax then, wouldn't you say?' Ivy asked.

'Perhaps.'

I paced back the other direction, my aspects growing silent. Finally, I heard the door shut below. I hurried to the landing down.

'Master?' Wilson said, climbing the steps.

'Wilson! Mail has arrived?'

He stopped at the landing, holding a silver tray. Megan, of

the cleaning staff – real, of course – scurried up behind him and passed us, face down, steps quick.

'She'll quit soon,' Ivy noted. 'You really should try to be less strange.'

'Tall order, Ivy,' I mumbled, looking through the mail. 'With you people around.' There! Another envelope, identical to the first. I tore into it eagerly and pulled out another picture.

This one was more blurry. It was of a man standing at a washbasin, towel at his neck. His surroundings were old-fashioned. It was also in black and white.

I turned the picture to Tobias. He took it, holding it up, inspecting it with eyes lined at the corners.

'Well?' Ivy asked.

'He looks familiar,' I said. 'I feel I should know him.'

'George Washington,' Tobias said. 'Having a morning shave, it appears. I'm surprised he didn't have someone to do it for him.'

'He was a soldier,' I said, taking the photo back. 'He was probably accustomed to doing things for himself.' I ran my fingers over the glossy picture. The first daguerreotype – early photographs – had been taken in the mid-1830s. Before that, nobody had been able to create permanent images of this nature. Washington had died in 1799.

'Look, this one is *obviously* a fake,' Ivy said. 'A picture of George Washington? We're to assume that someone went back in time, and the only thing they could think to do was grab a candid of George in the bathroom? We're being played, Steve.'

'Maybe,' I admitted.

'It does look *remarkably* like him,' Tobias said.

'Except we don't have any photos of him,' Ivy said. 'So there's no way to prove it. Look, all someone would have to do is hire a look-alike actor, pose the photo, and *bam*. They wouldn't even have to do any photo editing.'

'Let's see what Armando thinks,' I said, turning over the photo. On the back of this one was a phone number. 'Someone fetch Audrey first.'

'YOU MAY APPROACH His Majesty,' Armando said. He stood at his window, which was triangular – he occupied one of the peaks of the mansion. He'd demanded the position.

'Can I shoot him?' J.C. asked me softly. 'You know, in a place that's not important? A foot, maybe?'

'His Majesty heard that,' Armando said in his soft Spanish accent, turning unamused eyes our direction. 'Stephen Leeds. Have you fulfilled your promise to me? I must be restored to my throne.'

'Working on it, Armando,' I said, handing him the picture. 'We've got another one.'

Armando sighed, taking the photo from my fingers. He was a thin man with black hair he kept slicked back. 'Armando *benevolently* agrees to consider your supplication.' He held it up.

'You know, Steve,' Ivy said, poking through the room, 'if you're going to create hallucinations, you really should consider making them less annoying.'

'Silence, woman,' Armando said. 'Have you considered His Majesty's request?'

'I'm not going to marry you, Armando.'

'You would be queen!'

'You don't have a throne. And last I checked, Mexico has a president, not an emperor.'

'Drug lords threaten my people,' Armando said, inspecting the picture. 'They starve, and are forced to bow to the whims of foreign powers. It is a disgrace. This picture, it is authentic.' He handed it back.

'That's all?' I asked. 'You don't need to do some of those computer tests?'

'Am I not the photography expert?' Armando said. 'Did you not come to me with piteous supplication? I have spoken. It is real. No trickery. The photographer, however, is a buffoon. He knows nothing of the *art* of the craft. These pictures offend me in their utter pedestrian nature.' He turned his back to us, looking out the window again.

'*Now* can I shoot him?' J.C. asked.

'I'm tempted to let you,' I said, turning over the picture. Audrey had looked at the handwriting on the back, and hadn't been able to trace it to any of the professors, psychologists, or other groups that kept wanting to do studies on me.

I shrugged, then took out my phone. The number was local. It rang once before being picked up.

'Hello?' I said.

'May I come visit you, Mister Leeds?' A woman's voice, with a faint Southern accent.

'Who are you?'

'The person who has been sending you puzzles.'

'Well, I figured *that* part out.'

'May I come visit?'

'I ... well, I suppose. Where are you?'

'Outside your gates.' The phone clicked. A moment later, chimes rang as someone buzzed the front gates.

I looked at the others. J.C. pushed his way to the window, gun out, and peeked at the front driveway. Armando scowled at him.

Ivy and I walked out of Armando's rooms toward the steps.

'You armed?' J.C. asked, jogging up to us.

'Normal people don't walk around their own homes with a gun strapped on, J.C.'

'They do if they want to live. Go get your gun.'

I hesitated, then sighed. 'Let her in, Wilson!' I called, but redirected to my own rooms – the largest in the complex – and took my handgun out of my nightstand. I holstered it under my arm and put my jacket back on. It did feel good to be armed, but I'm a *horrible* shot.

By the time I was making my way down the steps to the front entryway, Wilson had answered the door. A dark-skinned woman in her thirties stood at the doorway, wearing a black jacket, a business suit, and short dreadlocks. She took off her sunglasses and nodded to me.

'The sitting room, Wilson,' I said, reaching the landing. He led her to it, and I entered after, waiting for J.C. and Ivy to pass. Tobias already sat inside, reading a history book.

'Lemonade?' Wilson asked.

'No, thank you,' I said, pulling the door closed, Wilson outside.

The woman strolled around the room, looking over the décor. 'Fancy place,' she said. 'You paid for all of this with money from people who ask you for help?'

'Most of it came from the government,' I said.

'Word on the street says you don't work for them.'

'I don't, but I used to. Anyway, a lot of this came from

grant money. Professors who wanted to research me. I started charging enormous sums for the privilege, assuming it would put them off.'

'And it didn't.'

'Nothing does,' I said, grimacing. 'Have a seat.'

'I'll stand,' she said, inspecting my Van Gogh. 'The name is Monica, by the way.'

'Monica,' I said, taking out the two photographs. 'I have to say, it seems remarkable that you'd expect me to believe your ridiculous story.'

'I haven't told you a story yet.'

'You're going to,' I said, tossing the photographs onto the table. 'A story about time travel and, apparently, a photographer who doesn't know how to use his flash properly.'

'You're a genius, Mister Leeds,' she said, not turning. 'By some certifications I've read, you're the smartest man on the planet. If there had been an obvious flaw – or one that wasn't so obvious – in those photos, you'd have thrown them away. You certainly wouldn't have called me.'

'They're wrong.'

'They … ?'

'The people who call me a genius,' I said, sitting down in the chair next to Tobias's. 'I'm not a genius. I'm really quite average.'

'I find that hard to believe.'

'Believe what you will,' I said. 'But I'm *not* a genius. My hallucinations are.'

'Thanks,' J.C. said.

'*Some* of my hallucinations are,' I corrected.

'You accept that the things you see aren't real?' Monica said, turning to me.

17

'Yes.'

'Yet you talk to them.'

'I wouldn't want to hurt their feelings. Besides, they can be useful.'

'Thanks,' J.C. said.

'*Some* of them can be useful,' I corrected. 'Anyway, they're the reason you're here. You want their minds. Now, tell me your story, Monica, or stop wasting my time.'

She smiled, finally walking over to sit down. 'It's not what you think. There's no time machine.'

'Oh?'

'You don't sound surprised.'

'Time travel into the past is highly, *highly* implausible,' I said. 'Even if it were to have occurred, I'd not know of it, as it would have created a branching path of reality of which I am not a part.'

'Unless this *is* the branched reality.'

'In which case,' I said, 'time travel into the past is still functionally irrelevant to me, as someone who traveled back would create a branching path of which – again – I would not be part.'

'That's one theory, at least,' she said. 'But it's meaningless. As I said, there is no time machine. Not in the conventional sense.'

'So these pictures are fakes?' I asked. 'You're starting to bore me very quickly, Monica.'

She slid three more pictures onto the table.

'Shakespeare,' Tobias said as I held them up one at a time. 'The Colossus of Rhodes. Oh … now that's clever.'

'Elvis?' I asked.

'Apparently the moment before death,' Tobias said, pointing

to the picture of the waning pop icon sitting in his bathroom, head drooping.

J.C. sniffed. 'As if there isn't anyone around who looks like *that guy*.'

'These are from a camera,' Monica said, leaning forward, 'that takes pictures of the past.'

She paused for dramatic effect. J.C. yawned.

'The problem with each of these,' I said, tossing the pictures onto the table, 'is that they are fundamentally unverifiable. They are pictures of things that have no other visual record to prove them, so therefore small inaccuracies would be impossible to use in debunking.'

'I have seen the device work,' Monica replied. 'It was proven in a rigorous testing environment. We stood in a clean room we had prepared, took cards and drew on the backs of them, and held them up. Then we burned the cards. The inventor of this device entered the room and took photos. Those pictures accurately displayed us standing there, with the cards and the patterns reproduced.'

'Wonderful,' I said. 'Now, if I only had any reason at all to trust your word.'

'You can test the device yourself,' she said. 'Use it to answer any question from history you wish.'

'We could,' Ivy said, 'if it hadn't been stolen.'

'I could do that,' I repeated, trusting what Ivy said. She had good instincts for interrogation, and sometimes fed me lines. 'Except the device has been stolen, hasn't it?'

Monica leaned back in her chair, frowning.

'It wasn't difficult to guess, Steve,' Ivy said. 'She wouldn't be here if everything were working properly, and she'd have brought the camera – to show it off – if she really wanted to prove it to us. I could believe it's in a lab somewhere, too valuable to bring. Only in that case, she'd have invited us to her center of strength, instead of coming to ours.

'She's desperate, despite her calm exterior. See how she keeps tapping the armrest of her chair? Also, notice how she tried to remain standing in the first part of the conversation, looming as if to prop up her authority? She only sat down when she felt awkward with you seeming so relaxed.'

Tobias nodded. '"Never do anything standing that you can do sitting, or anything sitting that you can do lying down." A Chinese proverb, usually attributed to Confucius. Of course, no primary texts from Confucius remain in existence, so nearly everything we attribute to him is guesswork, to some extent or another. Ironically, one of the only things we *are* sure he taught is the Golden Rule – and his quote regarding it is often misattributed to Jesus of Nazareth, who worded the same concept a different way ...'

I let him speak, the ebbs and flows of his calm voice washing across me like waves. What he was saying wasn't important.

'Yes,' Monica finally said. 'The device was stolen. And that is why I am here.'

'So we have a problem,' I said. 'The only way to prove these pictures authentic for myself would be to have the device. And yet, I can't have the device without doing the work you want me to do – meaning I could easily reach the end of this and discover you've been playing me.'

She dropped one more picture onto the table. A woman in sunglasses and a trench coat, standing in a train station. The picture had been taken from the side as she inspected a monitor above.

Sandra.

'Uh-oh,' J.C. said.

'Where did you get this?' I demanded, standing up.

'I've told you—'

'We're not playing games anymore!' I slammed my hands down on the coffee table. 'Where is she? What do you know?'

Monica drew back, eyes widening. People don't know how to handle schizophrenics. They've read stories, seen films. We make them afraid, though statistically we're not any more likely to commit violent crimes than the average person.

Of course, several people who wrote papers on me claim I'm *not* schizophrenic. Half think I'm making this all up. The other half think I've got something different, something new. Whatever I have – however it is that my brain works – only one person really ever seemed to *get* me. And that was the woman in the picture Monica had just slapped down on the table.

Sandra. In a way, she'd started all of this.

'The picture wasn't hard to get,' Monica said. 'When you used to do interviews, you would talk about her. Obviously, you hoped someone would read the interview and bring you information about her. Maybe you hoped that she would see what you had to say, and return to you ...'

I forced myself to sit back down.

'You knew she went to the train station,' Monica continued. 'And at what time. You didn't know which train she got on. We started taking pictures until we found her.'

'There must have been a dozen women in that train station with blonde hair and the right look,' I said.

Nobody really knew who she was. Not even me.

Monica took out a sheaf of pictures, a good twenty of them. Each was of a woman. 'We thought the one wearing sunglasses indoors was the most likely choice, but we took a shot of every woman near the right age in the train station that day. Just in case.'

Ivy rested a hand on my shoulder.

'Calmly, Stephen,' Tobias said. 'A strong rudder steers the ship even in a storm.'

I breathed in and out.

'Can I shoot *her*?' J.C. asked.

Ivy rolled her eyes. 'Remind me why we keep him around.'

'Rugged good looks,' J.C. said.

'Listen,' Ivy continued to me. 'Monica undermined her own story. She claims to have only come to you because the camera was stolen – yet how did she get pictures of Sandra without the camera?'

I nodded, clearing my head – with difficulty – and made the accusation to Monica.

Monica smiled slyly. 'We had you in mind for another project. We thought these would be ... handy to have.'

'Darn,' Ivy said, standing right up in Monica's face, focusing on her irises. 'I think she might be telling the truth on that one.'

I stared at the picture. Sandra. It had been almost ten years now. It *still* hurt to think about how she'd left me. Left me, after showing me how to harness my mind's abilities. I ran my fingers across the picture.

'We've got to do it,' J.C. said. 'We've got to look into this, skinny.'

'If there's a chance ...' Tobias said, nodding.

'The camera was probably stolen by someone on the inside,' Ivy guessed. 'Jobs like this one often are.'

'One of your own people took it, didn't they?' I asked.

'Yes,' Monica said. 'But we don't have any idea where they went. We've spent tens of thousands of dollars over the last four days trying to track them. I always suggested you. Other ... factions within our company were against bringing in someone they consider volatile.'

'I'll do it,' I said.

'Excellent. Shall I bring you to our labs?'

'No,' I said. 'Take me to the thief's house.'

'MISTER BALUBAL RAZON,' Tobias read from the sheet of facts as we climbed the stairs. I'd scanned that sheet on the drive over, but had been too deep in thought to give it much specific attention. 'He's ethnically Filipino, but second-generation American. Ph.D. in physics from the University of Maine. No honors. Lives alone.'

We reached the seventh floor of the apartment building. Monica was puffing. She kept walking too close to J.C., which made him scowl.

'I should add,' Tobias said, lowering the sheet of facts, 'Stan informs me that the rain has cleared up before reaching us. We have only sunny weather to look forward to now.'

'Thank goodness,' I said, turning to the door, where two men in black suits stood on guard. 'Yours?' I asked Monica, nodding to them.

'Yeah,' she said. She'd spent the ride over on the phone with some of her superiors.

Monica took out a key to the flat and turned it in the lock. The room inside was a complete disaster. Chinese take-out cartons stood on the windowsill in a row, as if planters intended to grow next year's crop of General Tso's. Books lay in piles everywhere, and the walls were hung with photographs. Not the time-traveling kind, just the ordinary photos a photography buff would take.

We had to shuffle around to get through the door and past the stacks of books. Inside, it was cramped quarters with all of us.

'Wait outside, if you will, Monica,' I said. 'It's kind of tight in here.'

'Tight?' she asked, frowning.

'You keep walking through the middle of J.C.,' I said. 'It's very disturbing for him; he hates being reminded he's a hallucination.'

'I'm not a hallucination,' J.C. snapped. 'I have state-of-the-art stealthing equipment.'

Monica regarded me for a moment, then walked to the doorway, standing between the two guards, hands on hips as she regarded us.

'All right, folks,' I said. 'Have at it.'

'Nice locks,' J.C. said, flipping one of the chains on the door. 'Thick wood, three deadbolts. Unless I miss my guess …' He poked at what appeared to be a letter box mounted on the wall by the door.

I opened it. There was a pristine handgun inside.

'Ruger Bisley, custom converted to large caliber,' J.C. said with a grunt. I opened the spinning thing that held the bullets and took one out. 'Chambered in .500 Linebaugh,' J.C. continued. 'This is a weapon for a man who knows what he's doing.'

'He left it behind, though,' Ivy said. 'Was he in too much of a hurry?'

'No,' J.C. said. 'This was his door gun. He had a different regular sidearm.'

'Door gun,' Ivy said. 'Is that really a *thing* for you people?'

'You need something with good penetration,' J.C. said, 'that can shoot through the wood when people are trying to force your door. But the recoil of this weapon will do a number on your hand after not too many shots. He would have carried something with a smaller caliber on his person.'

J.C. inspected the gun. 'Never been fired, though. Hmm … There's a chance someone gave this to him. Perhaps he went to a friend, asked them how to protect himself? A true soldier knows each weapon he owns through repeated firing. No gun fires perfectly straight. Each has a personality.'

'He's a scholar,' Tobias said, kneeling beside the rows of books. 'Historian.'

'You sound surprised,' I said. 'He *does* have a Ph.D. I'd expect him to be smart.'

'He has a Ph.D. in theoretical physics, Stephen,' Tobias said. 'But these are some *very* obscure historical and theological books. Deep reading. It's difficult to be a widely read scholar in more than one area. No wonder he leads a solitary life.'

'Rosaries,' Ivy said; she picked one up from the top of a stack of books, inspecting it. 'Worn, frequently counted. Open one of those books.'

I picked a book up off the floor.

'No, that one. *The God Delusion.*'

'Richard Dawkins?' I said, flipping through it.

'A leading atheist,' Ivy said, looking over my shoulder. 'Annotated with counterarguments.'

'A devout Catholic among a sea of secular scientists,' Tobias said. 'Yes … many of these works are religious or have religious connotations. Thomas Aquinas, Daniel W. Hardy, Francis Schaeffer, Pietro Alagona …'

'There's his badge from work,' Ivy said, nodding to something hanging on the wall. It proclaimed, in large letters, *Azari Laboratories, Inc.* Monica's company.

'Call for Monica,' Ivy said. 'Repeat what I tell you.'

'Oh Monica,' I said.

'Am I allowed in now?'

'Depends,' I said, repeating the words Ivy whispered to me. 'Are you going to tell me the truth?'

'About what?'

'About Razon having invented the camera on his own, bringing Azari in only after he had a working prototype.'

Monica narrowed her eyes at me.

'Badge is too new,' I said. 'Not worn or scratched at all from being used or in his pocket. The picture on it can't be more than two months old, judging by the beard he's growing in the badge photo but not in the picture of him at Mount Vernon on his mantle.

'Furthermore, this is *not* the apartment of a high-paid engineer. With a broken elevator? In the northeast quarter of town? Not only is this a rough area, it's too far from your offices. He didn't steal your camera, Monica – though I'm tempted to guess that you're trying to steal it from him. Is that why he ran?'

'He *didn't* come to us with a prototype,' Monica said. 'Not a working one, at least. He had one photo – the one of Washington – and a lot of promises. He needed money to get a stable machine working; apparently, the one he'd built had worked for a few days, then stopped.

'We funded him for eighteen months on a limited access pass to the labs. He received an official badge when he finally got the damn camera working. And he *did* steal it from us.

The contract he signed required all equipment to remain at our laboratories. He used us as a convenient source of cash, then jumped with the prize – wiping all of his data and destroying all other prototypes – as soon as he could get away with it.'

'Truth?' I asked Ivy.

'Can't tell,' she said. 'Sorry. If I could hear a heartbeat … maybe you could put your ear to her chest.'

'I'm sure she'd *love* that,' I said.

J.C. smiled. 'I'm pretty sure *I'd* love that.'

'Oh please,' Ivy said. 'You'd only do it to peek inside her jacket and find out what kind of gun she's carrying.'

'Beretta M9,' J.C. said. 'Already peeked.'

Ivy gave me a glare.

'What?' I said, trying to act innocent. 'He's the one who said it.'

'Skinny,' J.C. put in, 'the M9 is boring, but effective. The way she carries herself says she knows her way around a gun. That puffing she did when climbing the steps? An act. She's far more fit than that. She's trying to pretend she's some kind of manager or paper-pusher at the labs, but she's obviously security of some sort.'

'Thanks,' I told him.

'You,' Monica said, 'are a *very* strange man.'

I focused on her. She'd heard only my parts of the exchange, of course. 'I thought you read my interviews.'

'I did. They don't do you justice. I imagined you as a brilliant mode-shifter, slipping in and out of personalities.'

'That's dissociative identity disorder,' I said. 'It's different.'

'Very good!' Ivy piped in. She'd been schooling me on psychological disorders.

'Regardless,' Monica said. 'I guess I'm just surprised to find out what you really are.'

'Which is?' I asked.

'A middle manager,' she said, looking troubled. 'Anyway, the question remains. Where is Razon?'

'Depends,' I said. 'Does he need to be any place specific to use the camera? Meaning, did he have to *go* to Mount Vernon to take a picture of the past in that location, or can he somehow set the camera to take pictures there?'

'He has to go to the location,' Monica said. 'The camera looks back through time at the exact place you are.'

There were problems with that, but I let them slide for now. Razon. Where would he go? I glanced at J.C., who shrugged.

'You look to him first ?' Ivy said with a flat tone. 'Really.'

I looked to her, and she blushed. 'I ... I actually don't have anything either.'

J.C. chuckled at that.

Tobias stood up, slow and ponderous, like a distant cloud formation rising into the sky. 'Jerusalem,' he said softly, resting his fingers on a book. 'He's gone to Jerusalem.'

We all looked at him. Well, those of us who could.

'Where else would a believer go, Stephen?' Tobias asked. 'After years of arguments with his colleagues, years of being thought a fool for his faith? This was what it was about all along, this is why he developed the camera. He's gone to answer a question. For us, for himself. A question that has been asked for two thousand years.'

'He's gone to take a picture of Jesus of Nazareth – dubbed Christ by his devout – following his resurrection.'

I REQUIRED FIVE first-class seats. This did not sit well with Monica's superiors, many of whom did not approve of me. I met one of those at the airport, a Mr. Davenport. He smelled of pipe smoke, and Ivy critiqued his poor taste in shoes. I thought better of asking him if we could use the corporate jet.

We now sat in the first-class cabin of the plane. I flipped lazily through a thick book on my seat's fold-out tray. Behind me, J.C. bragged to Tobias about the weapons he'd managed to slip past security.

Ivy dozed by the window, with an empty seat next to her. Monica sat beside me, staring at that empty seat. 'So Ivy is by the window?'

'Yes,' I said, flipping a page.

'Tobias and the marine are behind us.'

'J.C.'s a Navy SEAL. He'd shoot you for making that mistake.'

'And the other seat?' she asked.

'Empty,' I said, flipping a page.

She waited for an explanation. I didn't give one.

'So what are you going to do with this camera?' I asked. 'Assuming the thing is real, a fact of which I'm not yet convinced.'

'There are hundreds of applications,' Monica said. 'Law enforcement ... Espionage ... Creating a true account of historical events ... Watching the early formation of the planet for scientific research ...'

'Destroying ancient religions ...'

She raised an eyebrow at me. 'Are you a religious man, then, Mister Leeds?'

'Part of me is.' That was the honest truth.

'Well,' she said. 'Let us assume that Christianity is a sham. Or, perhaps, a movement started by well-meaning people but which has grown beyond proportion. Would it not serve the greater good to expose that?'

'That's not really an argument I'm equipped to enter,' I said. 'You'd need Tobias. He's the philosopher. Of course, I think he's dozing.'

'Actually, Stephen,' Tobias said, leaning between our two seats, 'I'm quite curious about this conversation. Stan is watching our progress, by the way. He says there might be some bumpy weather up ahead.'

'You're looking at something,' Monica said.

'I'm looking at Tobias,' I said. 'He wants to continue the conversation.'

'Can I speak with him?'

'I suppose you can, through me. I'll warn you, though. Ignore anything he says about Stan.'

'Who's Stan?' Monica asked.

'An astronaut that Tobias hears, supposedly orbiting the world in a satellite.' I turned a page. 'Stan is mostly harmless. He gives us weather forecasts, that sort of thing.'

'I ... see,' she said. 'Stan's another one of your special friends?'

I chuckled. 'No. Stan's not real.'

'I thought you said none of them were.'

'Well, true. They're my hallucinations. But Stan is something special. Only Tobias hears him. Tobias is a schizophrenic.'

She blinked in surprise. 'Your hallucination ...'

'Yes?'

'Your hallucination has hallucinations.'

'Yes.'

She settled back, looking disturbed.

'They all have their issues,' I said. 'Ivy is a trypophobic, though she mostly has it under control. Just don't come at her with a wasp's nest. Armando is a megalomaniac. Adoline has OCD.'

'If you please, Stephen,' Tobias said. 'Let her know that I find Razon to be a very brave man.'

I repeated the words.

'And why is that?' Monica asked.

'To be both a scientist and religious is to create an uneasy truce within a man,' Tobias said. 'At the heart of science is accepting only that truth which can be proven. At the heart of faith is to define Truth, at its core, as being unprovable. Razon is a brave man because of what he is doing. Regardless of his discovery, one of two things he holds very dear will be upended.'

'He could be a zealot,' Monica replied. 'Marching blindly forward, trying to find final validation that he has been right all along.'

'Perhaps,' Tobias said. 'But the true zealot would not need validation. The Lord would provide validation. No, I see some-thing else here. A man seeking to meld science and faith, the first person – perhaps in the history of mankind – to *actually* find a way to apply science to the ultimate truths of religion. I find that noble.'

Tobias settled back. I flipped the last few pages of the book as Monica sat in thought. Finished, I stuffed the book into the pocket of the seat in front of me.

Someone rustled the curtains, entering from economy class and coming into the first-class cabin. 'Hello!' a friendly feminine voice said, walking up the aisle. 'I could not help seeing that you had an extra seat up here, and I thought to myself, perhaps they would let me sit in it.'

The newcomer was a round-faced, pleasant young woman in her late twenties. She had tan Indian skin and a deep red dot on her forehead. She wore clothing of intricate make, red and gold, with an Indian shawl-thingy over one shoulder and wrapping around her. I don't know what they're called.

'What's this?' J.C. said. 'Hey, Achmed. You're not going to blow the plane up, are you?'

'My name is Kalyani,' she said. 'And I am most certainly *not* going to blow anything up.'

'Huh,' J.C. said. 'That's disappointing.' He settled back and closed his eyes – or pretended to. He kept one eye cracked toward Kalyani.

'*Why* do we keep him around?' Ivy asked, stretching, coming out of her nap.

'Your head keeps going back and forth,' Monica said. 'I feel like I'm missing entire conversations.'

'You are,' I said. 'Monica, meet Kalyani. A new aspect, and the reason we needed that empty seat.'

Kalyani perkily held out her hand toward Monica, a big grin on her face.

'She can't see you, Kalyani,' I said.

'Oh, right!' Kalyani raised both hands to her face. 'I'm so sorry, Mister Steve. I am very new to this.'

'It's okay. Monica, Kalyani will be our interpreter in Israel.'

'I am a linguist,' Kalyani said, bowing.

'Interpreter …' Monica said, glancing at the book I'd tucked away. A book of Hebrew syntax, grammar, and vocabulary. 'You just learned Hebrew.'

'No,' I said. 'I glanced through the pages enough to summon

an aspect who speaks it. I'm useless with languages.' I yawned, wondering if there was time left in the flight to pick up Arabic for Kalyani as well.

'Prove it,' Monica said.

I raised an eyebrow toward her.

'I need to see,' Monica said. 'Please.'

With a sigh, I turned to Kalyani. 'How do you say: "I would like to practice speaking Hebrew. Would you speak to me in your language?"'

'Hm ... "I would like to practice speaking Hebrew" is somewhat awkward in the language. Perhaps, "I would like to improve my Hebrew"?'

'Sure.'

'Ani rotzeh leshapher et ha'ivrit sheli,' Kalyani said.

'Damn,' I said. 'That's a mouthful.'

'Language!' Ivy called.

'It is not so hard, Mister Steve. Here, try it. *Ani rotzeh leshapher et ha'ivrit sheli.'*

'Any rote zeele shaper hap ... er hav ...' I said.

'Oh my,' Kalyani said. 'That is ... that is very dreadful. Perhaps I will give you one word at a time.'

'Sounds good,' I said, waving over one of the flight attendants, the one who had spoken Hebrew to give the safety information at the start of our flight.

She smiled at us. 'Yes?'

'Uh ...' I said.

'Ani,' Kalyani said patiently.

'Ani,' I repeated.

'Rotzeh.'

'Rotzeh ...'

It took a little getting used to, but I made myself known.

The stewardess even congratulated me. Fortunately, translating her words into English was much easier – Kalyani gave me a running translation.

'Oh, your accent is *horrible*, Mister Steve,' Kalyani said as the stewardess moved on. 'I'm so embarrassed.'

'We'll work on it,' I said. 'Thanks.'

Kalyani smiled at me and gave me a hug, then tried to give one to Monica, who didn't notice. Finally, the Indian woman took a seat next to Ivy, and the two began chatting amicably, which was a relief. It always makes my life easier when my hallucinations get along.

'You already spoke Hebrew,' Monica accused. 'You knew it before we started flying, and you spent the last few hours refreshing yourself.'

'Believe that if you want.'

'But it's not *possible*,' she continued. 'A man can't learn an entirely new language in a matter of hours.'

I didn't bother to correct her and say I *hadn't* learned it. If I had, my accent wouldn't have been so horrible, and Kalyani wouldn't have needed to guide me word by word.

'We're on a plane hunting a camera that can take pictures of the past,' I said. 'How is it harder to believe that I just learned Hebrew?'

'Okay, fine. We'll pretend you did that. But if you're capable of learning that quickly, why don't you know every language – every subject, *everything* – by now?'

'There aren't enough rooms in my house for that,' I said. 'The truth is, Monica, I don't *want* any of this. I'd gladly be free of it, so that I could live a more simple life. I sometimes think the lot of them will drive me insane.'

'You ... aren't insane, then?'

'Heavens no,' I said. I eyed her. 'You don't accept that.'

'You see people who aren't there, Mister Leeds. It's a difficult fact to get around.'

'And yet, I live a good life,' I said. 'Tell me. Why would you consider me insane, but the man who can't hold a job, who cheats on his wife, who can't keep his temper in check? You call *him* sane?'

'Well, perhaps not completely ...'

'Plenty of "sane" people can't manage to keep it all under control. Their mental state – stress, anxiety, frustration – gets in the way of their ability to be happy. Compared to them, I think I'm downright stable. Though I do admit, it would be nice to be left alone. I don't want to be anyone special.'

'And that's where all of this came from, isn't it?' Monica asked. 'The hallucinations?'

'Oh, you're a psychologist now? Did you read a book on it while we were flying? Where's your new aspect, so I can shake hands with her?'

Monica didn't rise to the bait. 'You create these delusions so that you can foist things off on them. Your brilliance, which you find a burden. Your responsibility – they have to drag you along and make you help people. This lets you pretend, Mister Leeds. Pretend that you are normal. But that's the *real* delusion.'

I found myself wishing the flight would hurry up and be finished.

'I've never heard that theory before,' Tobias said softly from behind. 'Perhaps she has something, Stephen. We should mention it to Ivy—'

'No!' I snapped, turning on him. 'She's dug in my mind enough already.'

35

I turned back. Monica had that look in her eyes again, the look a 'sane' person gets when they deal with me. It's the look of a person forced to handle unstable dynamite while wearing oven mitts. That look … it hurts far more than the disease itself does.

'Tell me something,' I said to change the topic. 'How'd you let Razon get away with this?'

'It isn't like we didn't take precautions,' Monica said dryly. 'The camera was locked up tightly, but we couldn't very well keep it completely out of the hands of the man we were paying to build it.'

'There's more here,' I said. 'No offense intended, Monica, but you're a sneaky corporate type. Ivy and J.C. figured out ages ago that you're not an engineer. You're either a slimy executive tasked with handling undesirable elements, or you're a slimy security forces leader who does the same.'

'What part of that am I not supposed to take offense at?' she asked coolly.

'How did Razon have access to all of the prototypes?' I continued. 'Surely you copied the design without him knowing. Surely you fed versions of the camera to satellite studios, so they could break them apart and reverse engineer them. I find it quite a stretch to believe he somehow found and destroyed all of those.'

She tapped her armrest for a few minutes. 'None of them work,' she finally admitted.

'You copied the designs exactly?'

'Yes, but we got nothing from it. We asked Razon, and he said that there were still bugs. He always had an excuse, and Razon *did* have trouble with his own prototypes, after all. This is an area of science nobody has breached before. We're the pioneers. Things are bound to have bugs.'

'All true statements,' I said. 'None of which you believe.'

'He was doing *something* to those cameras,' she said. 'Something to make them stop functioning when he wasn't around. He could make any of the prototypes work, given enough time to fiddle. If we swapped in one of our copies during the night, he could make *it* function. Then we'd swap it back, and it wouldn't work for us.'

'Could other people use the cameras in his presence?'

She nodded. 'They could even use them for a little while when he wasn't there. Each camera would always stop working after a short time, and we'd have to bring him back in to fix it. You must understand, Mister Leeds. We only had a few months during which the cameras were working at all. For the majority of his career at Azari, he was considered a complete quack by most.'

'Not by you, I assume.'

She said nothing.

'Without him, without that camera, your career is nothing,' I said. 'You funded him. You championed him. And then, when it finally started working . . .'

'He betrayed me,' she whispered.

The look in her eyes was far from pleasant. It occurred to me that if we did find Mr. Razon, I might want to let J.C. at him first. J.C. would probably want to shoot the guy, but Monica wanted to rip him clean apart.

'WELL,' IVY SAID, 'it's a good thing we picked an out-of-the-way city. If we had to find Razon in a large urban center – home to three major world religions, one of the most

37

popular tourist destinations in the world – this would be *really* tough.'

I smiled as we walked out of the airport. One of Monica's two security goons went to track down the cars her company had ordered for us.

My smile didn't do much more than crack the corner of my lips. I hadn't gotten much study done on Arabic during the second half of the flight. I'd spent the time thinking about Sandra. That was never productive.

Ivy watched me from concerned eyes. She could be motherly sometimes. Kalyani strolled over to listen in on some people speaking in Hebrew nearby.

'Ah, Israel,' J.C. said, stepping up to us. 'I've always wanted to come over here, just to see if I could slip through security. They have the best in the world, you know.'

He carried a black duffle on his back that I didn't recognize. 'What's that?'

'M4A1 carbine,' J.C. said. 'With attached advanced combat optical gunsight and M203 grenade launcher.'

'But—'

'I have contacts over here,' he said softly. 'Once a SEAL, always a SEAL.'

The cars arrived, though the drivers seemed bemused at why four people insisted on two cars. As it was, they'd barely fit us all. I got into the second one, with Monica, Tobias, and Ivy – who sat between Monica and me in the back.

'Do you want to talk about it?' Ivy asked softly as she did up her seat belt.

'I don't think we'll find her, even with this,' I said. 'Sandra is good at avoiding attention, and the trail is too cold.'

Monica looked at me, a question on her lips, obviously

thinking I'd been talking to her. It died as she remembered whom she was accompanying.

'There might be a good reason why she left, you know,' Ivy said. 'We don't have the entire story.'

'A good reason? One that explains why, in ten years, she's never contacted us?'

'It's possible,' Ivy said.

I said nothing.

'You're not going to start losing us, are you?' Ivy asked. 'Aspects vanishing? Changing?'

Becoming nightmares. She didn't need to add that last part.

'That won't happen again,' I said. 'I'm in control now.'

Ivy still missed Justin and Ignacio. Honestly, I did too.

'And ... this hunt for Sandra,' Ivy said. 'Is it only about your affection for her, or is it about something else?'

'What else could it be about?'

'She was the one who taught you to control your mind.' Ivy looked away. 'Don't tell me you've never wondered. Maybe she has more secrets. A ... cure, perhaps.'

'Don't be stupid,' I said. 'I like things how they are.'

Ivy didn't reply, though I could see Tobias looking at me in the car's rearview mirror. Studying me. Judging my sincerity.

Honestly, I was judging my own.

What followed was a long drive to the city – the airport is quite a ways from the city proper. That was followed by a hectic ride through the streets of an ancient – yet modern – city. It was uneventful, save for us almost running over a guy selling olives. At our destination, we piled out of the cars, entering a sea of chattering tourists and pious pilgrims.

Built like a box, the building in front of us had an ancient, simple façade with two large, arched windows on the wall above us. 'The Church of the Holy Sepulchre,' Tobias said. 'Held by tradition to be the site of the crucifixion of Jesus of Nazareth, the structure *also* encloses one of the traditional locations of his burial. This marvelous structure was originally two buildings, constructed in the fourth century by order of Constantine the Great. It replaced a temple to Aphrodite that had occupied the same site for approximately two hundred years.'

'Thank you, Wikipedia,' J.C. grumbled, shouldering his assault rifle. He'd changed into combat fatigues.

'Whether tradition is correct,' Tobias continued calmly, hands clasped behind his back, 'and whether this is the *actual* location of the historical events, is a subject of some dispute. Though tradition has many convenient explanations for anomalies – such as reasoning that the temple to Aphrodite was constructed here to suppress early Christian worship – it has been shown that this church follows the shape of the pagan one in key areas. In addition, the fact that the church lies within the city walls makes for an excellent disputation, as the tomb of Jesus would have been outside the city.'

'It doesn't matter to us whether it is authentic or not,' I said, passing Tobias. 'Razon would have come here. It's one of the most obvious places – if not *the* most obvious place – to start looking. Monica, a word, please.'

She fell into step beside me, her goons going to check if we needed tickets to enter. The security here seemed very heavy – but, then, the church is in the West Bank, and there had been a couple of terrorist scares lately.

'What is it you want?' Monica asked me.

'Does the camera spit out pictures immediately?' I asked. 'Does it give digital results?'

'No. It takes pictures on film only. Medium format, no digital back. Razon insisted it be that way.'

'Now a harder one. You do realize the problems with a camera that takes pictures of one's very location, only farther back in time, don't you?'

'What do you mean?'

'Merely this: we're not in the same location now as we were two thousand years ago. The planet moves. One of the theoretical problems with time travel is that if you were to go back in time a hundred years to the exact point we're standing now, you'd likely find yourself in outer space. Even if you were extremely lucky – and the planet were in the exact same place in its orbit – the Earth's rotation would mean that you'd appear somewhere else on its surface. Or under its surface, or hundreds of feet in the air.'

'That's ridiculous.'

'It's science,' I said, looking up at the face of the church. *What we're doing here is ridiculous.*

And yet ...

'All I know,' she said, 'is that Razon had to go to a place to take pictures of it.'

'All right,' I said. 'One more. What's he like? Personality?'

'Abrasive,' she said immediately. 'Argumentative. And he is *very* protective of his equipment. I'm sure half of the reason he got away with the camera was because he'd repeatedly convinced us he was OCD with his stuff, so we gave him too much leniency.'

Eventually, our group made its way into the church. The stuffy air carried the sounds of whispering tourists and feet shuffling on the stones. It was still a functioning place of worship.

'We're missing something, Steve,' Ivy said, falling into step beside me. 'We're ignoring an important part of the puzzle.'

'Any guesses?' I asked, looking over the highly ornamented insides of the church.

'I'm working on it.'

'Wait,' J.C. said, sauntering up. 'Ivy, you think we're missing something, but you don't know what it is, and have no clue what it might be?'

'Basically,' Ivy said.

'Hey, skinny,' he said to me, 'I think I'm missing a million dollars, but I don't know why, or have any clue as to how I might have earned it. But I'm *really* sure I'm missing it. So if you could do something about that ...'

'You are such a buffoon,' Ivy said.

'That there, that thing I said,' J.C. continued, 'that was a *metaphor.*'

'No,' she said, 'it was a logical proof.'

'Huh?'

'One intended to demonstrate that you're an idiot. Oh! Guess what? The proof was a success! *Quod erat demonstrandum.* We can accurately say, without equivocation, that you are, indeed, an idiot.'

The two of them walked off, continuing the argument. I shook my head, moving deeper into the church. The place where the crucifixion had supposedly taken place was marked by a gilded alcove, congested with both tourists and the devout. I folded my arms, displeased. Many of the tourists were taking photographs.

'What?' Monica asked me.

'I'd hoped they'd forbid flash photography,' I said. 'Most places like this do.' If Razon had tried to use his, it would have made it more likely that someone had spotted him.

Perhaps it was forbidden, but the security guards standing nearby didn't seem to care what people did.

'We'll start looking,' Monica said, gesturing curtly to her men. The three of them moved through the crowd, going about our fragile plan – which was to try to find someone at one of the holy sites who remembered seeing Razon.

I waited, noticing that a couple of the security guards nearby were chatting in Hebrew. One waved to the other, apparently going off duty, and began to walk away.

'Kalyani,' I said. 'With me.'

'Of course, of course, Mister Steve.' She joined me with a hop in her step as we walked up to the departing guard.

The guard gave me a tired look.

'*Hello,*' I said in Hebrew with Kalyani's help. I'd first mutter under my breath what I wanted to say, so she could translate it for me. '*I apologize for my terrible Hebrew!*'

He paused, then smiled. '*It's not so bad.*'

'*It's dreadful.*'

'*You are Jewish?*' he guessed. '*From the States?*'

'*Actually, I'm not Jewish, though I am from the States. I just think a man should try to learn a country's language before he visits.*'

The guard smiled. He seemed an amiable enough fellow; of course, most people were. And they liked to see foreigners trying their own language. We chatted some more as he walked, and I found that he was indeed going off duty. Someone was coming to pick him up, but he didn't seem to mind talking to me while he waited. I tried to make it obvious that I wanted to practice my language by speaking with a native.

His name was Moshe, and he worked this same shift almost

every day. His job was to watch for people doing stupid things, then stop them – though he confided that his more important duty was to make sure no terrorist strikes happened in the church. He was extra security, not normal staff, hired for the holidays, when the government worried about violence and wanted a more visible presence in tourist sites. This church was, after all, in contested territory.

A few minutes in, I started moving the conversation toward Razon. *'I'm sure you must see some interesting things,'* I said. *'Before we came here, we were at the Garden Tomb. There was this crazy Asian guy there, yelling at everybody.'*

'Yeah?' Moshe asked.

'Yeah. Pretty sure he was American from his accent, but he had Asian features. Anyway, he had this big camera set up on a tripod – as if he were the most important person around, and nobody else deserved to take pictures. Got in this big argument with a guard who didn't want him using his flash.'

Moshe laughed. *'He was here too.'*

Kalyani chuckled after translating that. 'Oh, you're *good*, Mister Steve.'

'Really?' I asked, casually.

'Sure was,' Moshe said. *'Must be the same guy. He was here . . . oh, two days back. Kept cursing out everyone who jostled him, tried to bribe me to move them all away and give him space. Thing is, when he started taking pictures, he didn't mind if anyone stepped in front of him. And he took shots all over the church, even outside, pointed at the dumbest locations!'*

'Real loon, eh?'

'Yes,' the guard said, chuckling. *'I see tourists like him all the time. Big fancy cameras that they spent a ridiculous amount on, but they don't have a bit of photography training. This guy, he didn't*

*know when to turn off his flash, you know? Used it on every shot –
even out in the sun, and on the altar over there, with all the lights
on it!'*

I laughed.

'I know!' he said. *'Americans!'* Then he hesitated. *'Oh, uh, no
offense meant.'*

'None taken,' I said, relaying immediately what Kalyani said
in response. *'I'm Indian.'*

He hesitated, then cocked his head at me.

'Oh!' Kalyani said. 'Oh, I'm sorry, Mister Steve! I wasn't
thinking.'

'It's all right.'

The guard laughed. *'You are good at Hebrew, but I do not
think that means what you think!'*

I laughed as well, and noticed a woman moving toward
him, waving. I thanked him for the conversation, then inspected the church some more. Monica and her flunkies eventually found me, one of them tucking away some photos of
Razon. 'Nobody here has seen him, Leeds,' she said. 'This is
a dead end.'

'Is that so?' I asked, strolling toward the exit.

Tobias joined us, hands clasped behind his back. 'Such a
marvel, Stephen,' he said to me. He nodded toward an armed
guard at the doorway. 'Jerusalem, a city whose name literally
means "peace." It is filled with islands of serenity like this one,
which have seen the solemn worship of men for longer than
most countries have existed. Yet here, violence is never more
than a few steps away.'

Violence . . .

'Monica,' I said, frowning. 'You said you'd searched for
Razon on your own, before you came to me. Did that include

checking to see if he was on any flights out of the States?'

'Yeah,' she said. 'We have some contacts in Homeland Security. Nobody by Razon's name flew out of the country, but false IDs aren't *that* hard to find.'

'Could a fake passport get you into Israel? One of the most secure countries on the planet?'

She frowned. 'I hadn't thought of that.'

'It seems risky,' I said.

'Well, this is a fine time to bring it up, Leeds. Are you saying he's not here after all? We've wasted—'

'Oh, he's here,' I said absently. 'I found a guard who spoke to him. Razon took pictures all over the place.'

'Nobody we talked to saw him.'

'The guards and clergy in this place see *thousands* of visitors a day, Monica. You can't show them a picture and expect them to remember. You have to focus on something memorable.'

'But—'

'Hush for a moment,' I said, holding up my hand. *He got into the country. A mousy little engineer with extremely valuable equipment, using a fake passport. He had a gun back at his apartment, but hadn't ever fired it. How did he get it?*

Idiot. 'Can you find out when Razon bought that gun?' I asked her. 'Gun laws in the state should make it traceable, right?'

'Sure. I'll look into it when we get to a hotel.'

'Do it now.'

'Now? Do you realize what time it is in the—'

'Do it anyway. Wake people. Get the answers.'

She glared at me, but moved off and made a few phone calls. Some angry conversations followed.

'We should have seen this earlier,' Tobias said, shaking his head.

'I know.'

Eventually, Monica moved back, slapping closed her phone. 'There is no record of Razon buying a gun, ever. The one in his apartment isn't registered anywhere.'

He had help. Of *course* he had help. He'd been planning this for years, and he had access to all those photos to use in proving that he was legitimate.

He'd found someone to supply him. Protect him. Someone who had given him that gun, some fake identification. They'd helped him sneak into Israel.

So whom had he approached? Who was helping him?

'Ivy,' I said. 'We need . . .' I trailed off. 'Where's Ivy?'

'No idea,' Tobias said. Kalyani shrugged.

'You've *lost* one of your hallucinations?' Monica asked.

'Yes.'

'Well, summon her back.'

'It doesn't work that way,' I said, and poked through the church, looking around. I got some funny looks from clergy until I finally peeked into a nook and stopped flat.

J.C. and Ivy hastily broke apart from their kissing. Her makeup was mussed, and – incredibly – J.C. had set his gun to the side, ignoring it. That was a first.

'Oh, you've got to be *kidding* me,' I said, raising a hand to my face. '*You two?* What are you doing?'

'I wasn't aware we had to report the nature of our relationship to you,' Ivy said coldly.

J.C. gave me a big thumbs-up and a grin.

'Whatever,' I said. 'Time to go. Ivy, I don't think Razon was working alone. He came into the country on a fake passport, and other factors don't add up. Could he have had some sort of aid here? Maybe a local organization to help him escape suspicion and move in the city?'

'Possible,' she said, hurrying to keep up. 'I would point out it's not *impossible* that he's working alone, but it does seem unlikely, upon consideration. You thought that through on your own? Nice work!'

'Thanks. And your hair is a mess.'

We eventually reached the cars and climbed in, me with Monica, Ivy, and J.C. The two suits and my other aspects took the forward car.

'You could be right on this point,' Monica said as the cars started off.

'Razon is a smart man,' I said. 'He would have wanted allies. It could be another company, perhaps an Israeli one. Do any of your rivals know about this technology?'

'Not that we know of.'

'Steve,' Ivy said, sitting between us. She put her lipstick away, her hair fixed. She was obviously trying to ignore what I'd seen between her and J.C.

Damn, I thought. I'd assumed the two *hated* each other. *Think about that later.* 'Yes?' I asked.

'Ask Monica something for me. Did Razon ever approach her company about a project like this? Taking photos to prove Christianity?'

I relayed the question.

'No,' Monica said. 'If he had, I'd have told you. It would have led us here faster. He never came to us.'

'That's an oddity,' Ivy said. 'The more we work on this case, the more we find that Razon went to incredible lengths in order to come here, to Jerusalem. Why not use the resource he already had? Azari Laboratories.'

'Maybe he wanted freedom,' I said. 'To use his invention as he wished.'

'If that's the case,' Ivy said, 'he wouldn't have approached a rival company, as you proposed. Doing so would have put him back in the same situation. Prod Monica. She looks like she's thinking about something.'

'What?' I asked Monica. 'You have something to add?'

'Well,' Monica said, 'once we knew the camera was working, Razon *did* ask us about some projects he wanted to attempt. Revealing the truth of the Kennedy assassination, debunking or verifying the Patterson-Gimlin bigfoot video, things like that.'

'And you shot him down,' I guessed.

'I don't know if you've spent much time considering the ramifications of this device, Mister Leeds,' Monica said. 'Your questions to me on the plane indicate you've at least started to. Well, we have. And we're terrified.

'This thing will change the world. It's about more than proving mysteries. It means an end to privacy as we know it. If someone can gain access to *any* place where you have *ever* been naked, they can take photos of you in the nude. Imagine the ramifications for the paparazzi.

'Our entire justice system will be upended. No more juries, no more judges, lawyers, or courts. Law enforcement will simply need to go to the scene of the crime and take photos. If you're suspected, you provide an alibi – and they can prove whether or not you were where you claim.'

She shook her head, looking haunted. 'And what of history? National security? Secrets become much harder to keep. States will have to lock down sites where important information was once presented. You won't be able to write things down. A courier carrying sensitive documents has passed down the street? The next day, you can get into just the right position and take a picture *inside* the envelope. We tested that. Imagine having such power. Now imagine every person on the planet having it.'

'Dang,' Ivy whispered.

'So no,' Monica said. 'No, we wouldn't have let Mister Razon go and take photos to prove or disprove Christianity. Not yet. Not until we'd done a *lot* of discussion about the matter. He knew this, I think. It explains why he ran.'

'That didn't stop you from preparing ways to bait me into entering into a business arrangement with you,' I said. 'I suspect if you did it for me, you did it for other important people as well. You've been gathering resources to get yourself some strategic allies, haven't you? Maybe some of the world's rich and elite? To help you ride this wave, once the technology goes out?'

She drew her lips into a line, eyes straight forward.

'That probably looked self-serving to Razon,' I said. 'You won't help him with bringing the truth to mankind, but you'll gather bribery material? Even blackmail material.'

'I'm not at liberty to continue this conversation,' Monica said.

Ivy sniffed. 'Well, we know why he left. I still don't think he'd have gone to a rival company, but he would have gone to *someone*. The Israeli government, maybe? Or—'

Everything went black.

❧

I AWOKE, DAZED. My vision was blurry.

'Explosion,' J.C. said. He crouched beside me. I was …
I was tied up somewhere. In a chair. Hands bound behind
me.

'Stay calm, skinny,' J.C. said. '*Calm*. They blew the car in
front of us. We swerved. Hit a building at the side of the road.
Do you remember?'

I barely did. It was vague.

'Monica?' I croaked, looking about.

She was tied to a chair beside me. Kalyani, Ivy, and Tobias
were there as well, tied and gagged. Monica's security men
weren't there.

'I managed to crawl free of the wreckage,' J.C. said. 'But I
can't get you out.'

'I know,' I said. It was best not to push J.C. on the fact that
he was a hallucination. I'm pretty sure he knew, deep down,
exactly what he was. He just didn't like admitting it.

'Listen,' J.C. said. 'This is a bad situation, but you *will* keep
your head, and you *will* escape alive. Understand, soldier?'

'Yeah.'

'Say it again.'

'*Yes*,' I said, quiet but intense.

'Good man,' J.C. said. 'I'm going to go untie the others.' He
moved over, letting my other aspects free.

Monica groaned, shaking her head. 'What …'

'I think we've made a gross miscalculation,' I said. 'I'm
sorry.'

I was surprised at how evenly that came out, considering
how terrified I was. I'm an academic at heart – at least, most
of my aspects are. I'm not good with violence.

'What do you see?' I asked. This time, my voice quivered.

'Small room,' Ivy said, rubbing her wrists. 'No windows. I

can hear plumbing and faint sounds of traffic outside. We're still in the city.'

'Such lovely places you take us, Stephen,' Tobias said, nodding in thanks as J.C. helped him to his feet. Tobias was getting on in years, now.

'That's Arabic we hear,' Kalyani said. 'And I smell spices. Za'atar, saffron, turmeric, sumac ... We are near a restaurant, maybe?'

'Yes ...' Tobias said, eyes closed. 'Soccer stadium, distant. A passing train. Slowing. Stopping ... Cars, people talking. A mall?' He snapped his eyes open. 'Malha Railway Station. It's the only station in the city near a soccer stadium. This is a busy area. Screaming might draw help.'

'Or might get us killed,' J.C. said. 'Those ropes are tight, skinny. Monica's are too.'

'What's going on?' Monica asked. 'What happened?'

'The pictures,' Ivy said.

I looked at her.

'Monica and her goons showed off those pictures of Razon, walking around the church,' Ivy said. 'They probably asked every person there if they'd seen him. If he *was* working with someone ...'

I groaned. Of course. Razon's allies would have been watching for anyone hunting him. Monica had drawn a big red bull's-eye on us.

'All right,' I said. 'J.C. You're going to have to get us out of this. What should—'

The door opened.

I immediately turned toward our captors. I didn't find what I'd expected. Instead of Islamic terrorists of some sort, we were faced by a group of Filipino men in suits.

'Ah …' Tobias said.

'Mister Leeds,' said the man in the front, speaking with an accented voice. He flipped through a folder full of papers. 'By all accounts, you are a very interesting and very … reasonable person. We apologize for your treatment so far, and would like to see you placed in much more comfortable conditions.'

'I sense a deal coming on,' Ivy warned.

'I am called Salic,' the man said. 'I represent a certain group with interests that may align with your own. Have you heard of the MNLF, Mister Leeds?'

'The Moro National Liberation Front,' Tobias said. 'It is a Filipino revolutionary group seeking to split off and create its own nation-state.'

'I've heard of it,' I said.

'Well,' Salic said. 'I have a proposal for you. We have the device for which you are searching, but we have run into some difficulties in operating it. How much would it cost us to enlist your aid?'

'One million, US,' I said without missing a beat.

'Traitor!' Monica sputtered.

'You aren't even paying me, Monica,' I said, amused. 'You can't blame me for taking a better deal.'

Salic smiled. He fully believed I'd sell out Monica. Sometimes it is very useful to have a reputation for being a reclusive, amoral jerk.

The thing is, I'm really only the reclusive part. And maybe, admittedly, the jerk part. When you have that mix, people generally assume you don't have morals either.

'The MNLF is a paramilitary organization,' Tobias continued. 'There hasn't been much in the way of violence on their part, however, so this is surprising to see. Their fundamental difference with the main Filipino government is over religion.'

'Isn't it always?' J.C. said with a grunt, inspecting the newcomers for weapons. 'This guy is packing,' he said, nodding to the leader. 'I think they all are.'

'Indeed,' Tobias said. 'Think of the MNLF as the Filipino version of the IRA, or Palestine's own Hamas. The latter may be a more accurate comparison, as the MNLF is often seen as an Islamic organization. Most of the Philippines is Roman Catholic, but the Bangsamoro region – where the MNLF operates – is predominantly Islamic.'

'Untie him,' Salic said, gesturing toward me.

His men got to work.

'He's lying about something,' Ivy said.

'Yes,' Tobias said. 'I think ... Yes, he's not MNLF. He's perhaps trying to pin this on them. Stephen, the MNLF is *very much* against endangering civilians. It's really quite remarkable, if you read about them. They are freedom fighters, but they have a strict code of whom they'll hurt. They have recently been dedicated to peaceful secession.'

'That must not make them terribly popular with all who would follow them,' I said. 'Are there splinter groups?'

'What is that?' Salic asked.

'Nothing,' I said, standing up, rubbing my wrists. 'Thank you. I would *very much* like to see the device.'

'This way, please,' Salic said.

'Bastard,' Monica called after me.

'Language!' Ivy said, pursing her lips. She and my other aspects followed me out, and the guards shut the door on Monica, leaving her alone in the room.

'Yes ...' Tobias said, walking behind the men who escorted

me up the steps. 'Stephen, I think this is the Abu Sayyaf. Led by a man named Khadaffy Janjalani, they split from the MNLF because the organization wasn't willing to go far enough. Janjalani died recently, and the future of the movement is somewhat in doubt, but his goal was to create a purely Islamic state in the region. He considered the killing of anyone opposed to him as an ... elegant way to achieve his goals.'

'Sounds like we have a winner,' J.C. said. 'All right, skinny. Here's what you need to do. Kick the guy behind you as he's taking a step. He'll fall into the fellow next to him, and you can tackle Salic. Spin him around to cover gunfire from behind, take his weapon from inside his coat, and start firing through his body at the men down there.'

Ivy looked sick. 'That's awful!'

'You don't think he's going to let us go, do you?' J.C. asked.

'The Abu Sayyaf,' Tobias said helpfully, 'has been the source of numerous killings, bombings, and kidnappings in the Philippines. They also are *very* brutal with the locals, acting as more of an organized crime family than true revolutionaries.'

'So ... that would be a no, eh?' J.C. said.

We reached the ground floor, and Salic led us into a side room. Two more men were here, outfitted as soldiers, with grenades on their belts and assault rifles in their hands.

Between them, on the table, was a medium format camera. It looked ... ordinary.

'I need Razon here,' I said, sitting down. 'To ask him questions.'

Salic sniffed. 'He will not speak to you, Mister Leeds. You can trust us on this count.'

'So he's not working with them?' J.C. asked. 'I'm confused.'

'Bring him anyway,' I said, and carefully began prodding at the camera.

Thing is, I had *no* idea what I was doing. *Why, WHY didn't I bring Ivans with me?* I should have known I'd need a mechanic on this trip.

But if I brought too many aspects – kept too many of them around me at once – bad things happened. That was immaterial, now. Ivans was a continent away.

'Anyone?' I asked under my breath.

'Don't look at me,' Ivy said. 'I can't get the remote control to work half the time.'

'Cut the red wire,' J.C. said. 'It's always the red wire.'

I gave him a flat stare, then unscrewed one part of the camera in an attempt to look like I knew what I was doing. My hands were shaking.

Salic, fortunately, sent someone to do as I requested. After that, he watched me carefully. He'd probably read about the Longway Incident, where I'd disassembled, fixed, and reassembled a complex computer system in time to stop a detonation. But that had all been Ivans, with some aid by Chin, our resident computer expert.

Without them, I was useless at this sort of thing. I tried my best to look otherwise until the soldier brought back Razon. I recognized him from the pictures Monica had shown me. Barely. His lip was cracked and bleeding, his left eye puffy, and he walked with a stumbling limp. As he sat down on a stool near me, I saw that he was missing one hand. The stump was wrapped with a bloody rag.

He coughed. 'Ah. Mister Leeds, I believe,' he said with a faint Filipino accent. 'I'm terribly sorry to find you here.'

'Careful,' Ivy said, inspecting Razon. She was standing

right beside him. 'They're watching. Don't act too friendly.'

'Oh, I do *not* like this at all,' Kalyani said. She'd moved over to some crates at the back of the room, crouching down for cover. 'Is it often going to be like this around you, Mister Steve? Because I am not very well cut out for this.'

'You're *sorry* to find me here?' I said to Razon, making my voice harsh. 'Sorry, but not surprised. You're the one who helped Monica and her cronies get blackmail material on me.'

His unswollen eye widened a fraction. He knew it hadn't been blackmail material. Or so I hoped. Would he see? Would he realize I was here to help him?

'I did that ... under duress,' he said.

'You're still a bastard, so far as I'm concerned,' I spat.

'Language!' Ivy said, hands on hips.

'Bah,' I said to Razon. 'It doesn't matter. You're going to show me how to make this machine work.'

'I will not!' he said.

I turned a screw, my mind racing. How could I get close enough to speak to him quietly, but not draw suspicion? 'You will, or—'

'Careful, you fool!' Razon said, leaping from his chair.

One of the soldiers leveled a gun at us.

'Safety's on,' J.C. said. 'Nothing to be worried about. Yet.'

'This is a very delicate piece of equipment,' Razon said, taking the screwdriver from me. 'You mustn't break it.' He started screwing with his good arm. Then, speaking very softly, he continued. 'You are here with Monica?'

'Yes.'

'She is not to be trusted,' he said. Then paused. 'But she

never beat me or cut my hand off. So perhaps I am not one to speak on whom to trust.'

'How did they take you?' I whispered.

'I bragged to my mother,' he said. 'And she bragged to her family. It got to these monsters. They have contacts in Israel.' He wavered, and I reached to steady him. His face was pale. This man was *not* in good shape.

'They sent to me,' he said, forcing himself to keep screwing. 'They claimed to be Christian fundamentalists from my country, eager to fund my operation to find proof. I did not find out the truth until two days ago. It—'

He cut off, dropping the screwdriver as Salic stepped closer to us. The terrorist waved, and one of his soldiers grabbed Razon and jerked him back by his bloodied arm. Razon cried out in pain.

The soldiers proceeded to throw him to the ground and beat him with the butts of their rifles. I watched in horror, and Kalyani began crying. Even J.C. turned away.

'I am not a monster, Mister Leeds,' Salic said, squatting down beside my chair. 'I am a man with few resources. You will find that the two are quite difficult to differentiate, in most situations.'

'Please stop the soldiers,' I whispered.

'I am *trying* to find a peaceful solution, you see,' Salic said. He did not stop the beating. 'My people are condemned when we use the only methods we have – the methods of the desperate – to fight. These are the methods that every revolutionary, including the founders of your own country, has used to gain freedom. We will kill if we have to, but perhaps we do not have to. Here on this table we have peace, Mister Leeds. Fix this machine, and you will save thousands upon thousands of lives.'

'Why do you want it?' I said, frowning. 'What is it to you? Power to blackmail?'

'Power to fix the world,' Salic said. 'We just need a few photos. Proof.'

'Proof that Christianity is false, Stephen,' Tobias said, walking up beside me. 'That will be a difficult task for them, as Islam accepts Jesus of Nazareth as a prophet. They do not accept the resurrection, however, or many of the miracles attributed to later followers. With the right photo, they could try to undermine Catholicism – the religion followed by most Filipinos – and therefore destabilize the region.'

I'll admit that, strangely, I was tempted. Oh, not tempted to help a monster like Salic. But I did see his point. Why not take this camera, prove *all* religions false?

It would cause chaos. Perhaps a great deal of death, in some parts of the world.

Or would it?

'Faith is not so easily subverted,' Ivy said dismissively. 'This wouldn't cause the problems he thinks it would.'

'Because faith is blind?' Tobias asked. 'Perhaps you are right. Many would continue to believe, despite the facts.'

'What facts?' Ivy said. 'Some pictures that may or may not be trustworthy? Produced by a science nobody understands?'

'Already you try to protect that which has yet to be discounted,' Tobias said calmly. 'You act as if you know what will happen, and need to be defensive about the proof that *may* be found. Ivy, don't you see? What facts would it take to make you look at things with rational eyes? How can you be so logical in so many areas, yet be so blind in this one?'

'Quiet!' I said to them. I raised my hands to my head. 'Quiet!'

Salic frowned at me. Only then did he notice what his soldiers had done to Razon.

He shouted something in Tagalog, or perhaps one of the other Filipino languages – maybe I should have studied those instead of Hebrew. The soldiers backed away, and Salic knelt to roll over the fallen Razon.

Razon snapped his good hand into Salic's jacket, reaching for the gun. Salic jumped back, and one of the soldiers cried out. A single quiet *click* followed.

Everyone in the room grew still. One of the soldiers had taken out a handgun with a suppressor on it and shot Razon in a panic. The scientist lay back, dead eyes staring open, Salic's handgun slipping from his fingers.

'Oh, that poor man,' Kalyani said, moving over to kneel beside him.

At that moment, someone tackled one of the soldiers by the door, pulling him down from behind.

Shouting began immediately. I jumped out of my chair, reaching for the camera. Salic got it first, slamming one hand down on it, then reached toward his gun on the floor.

I cursed, scrambling away, throwing myself behind the stack of crates where Kalyani had taken cover a few moments before. Gunfire erupted in the room, and one of the crates near me threw up chips as a shot hit it.

'It's Monica!' Ivy said, taking cover beside the desk. 'She got out, and she's attacking them.'

I dared peek around, in time to see one of the Abu Sayyaf suits fall to gunfire, toppling in the center of the room near Razon's body. The others fired at Monica, who'd taken cover in the stairwell that led down to where we'd been captive.

'Holy hell!' J.C. said, crouching beside me. 'She escaped

on her own. I think I might have to start liking that woman!'

Salic yelled in Tagalog. He hadn't come after me, but had taken cover near his guards. He clutched the camera close, and was joined by two other soldiers as they ran down the stairs from above.

This gunfire would draw attention soon, I guessed. Not soon enough. They had Monica pinned. I could barely see her, hiding in her stairwell, trying to find a way to get out and fire on the men with the weapon she'd stolen from the guard she'd tackled. His feet stuck out of the doorway near her.

'Okay, skinny,' J.C. said. 'This is your chance. Something has to be done. They'll get her before help comes, and we lose the camera. It's hero time.'

'I ...'

'You could run, Stephen,' Tobias said. 'There's a room right behind us. There will be windows. I'm not saying you should do it; I'm giving you the options.'

Kalyani whimpered, huddled down in the corner. Ivy lay under a table, fingers in her ears, watching the fire-fight with calculating eyes.

Monica tried to duck out and fire, but bullets tore into the wall beside her, forcing her back. Salic was still yelling something. Several of the soldiers started firing on me, driving me back under cover.

Bullets popped against the wall above me, chips of stone dropping on my head. I breathed in and out. 'I can't do this, J.C.'

'You can,' he said. 'Look, they're carrying grenades. Did you see those on the belts of the soldiers? One will get smart, toss one of those down the stairwell, and Monica's gone. Dead.'

If I let them keep the camera – that kind of power, in the hands of men like this …

Monica yelled.

'She's hit!' Ivy called.

I scrambled out from behind the crates and ran for the fallen soldier at the center of the room. He'd dropped a hand-gun. Salic noticed me as I grabbed the weapon and raised it. My hands shook, quivering.

This is never going to work. I can't do this. It's impossible.

I'm going to die.

'Don't worry, kid,' J.C. said, taking my wrist in his own. 'I've got this.'

He pulled my arm to the side and I fired, barely looking, then he moved the gun in a series of motions, pausing just briefly for me to pull the trigger each time. It was over in moments.

Each of the armed men dropped. The room went completely still. J.C. released my wrist, and my arm fell leaden at my side.

'Did *we* do that?' I asked, looking at the fallen men.

'Damn,' Ivy said, unplugging her ears. 'I *knew* there was a reason we kept you around, J.C.'

'Language, Ivy,' he said, grinning.

I dropped the pistol – probably not the smartest thing I've ever done, but then again, I wasn't exactly in my right mind. I hurried to Razon's side. He had no pulse. I closed his eyes, but left the smile on his lips.

This was what he'd wanted. He'd wanted them to kill him so that he couldn't be forced to give up his secrets. I sighed. Then, checking a theory, I shoved my hand into his pocket.

Something pricked my fingers, and I brought them out bloodied. 'What ... ?'

I hadn't expected *that*.

'Leeds?' Monica's voice said.

I looked up. She was standing in the doorway to the room, holding her shoulder, which was bloodied. 'Did *you* do this?'

'J.C. did it,' I said.

'Your hallucination? Shot these men?'

'Yes. No. I ...' I wasn't sure. I stood up and walked over to Salic, who had been hit square in the forehead. I leaned down and picked up the camera, then twisted one piece of it, my back to Monica.

'Uh ... Mister Steve?' Kalyani said, pointing. 'I do not think that one is dead. Oh my.'

I looked. One of the guards I'd shot was turning over. He held something in a bloodied hand.

A grenade.

'Out!' I yelled at Monica, grabbing her by the arm as I charged out of the room.

The detonation hit me from behind like a crashing wave.

EXACTLY ONE MONTH later, I sat in my mansion, drinking a cup of lemonade. My back ached, but the shrapnel wounds were healing. It hadn't been that bad.

Monica did not give the cast on her arm much notice. She held her own cup, seated in the room where I'd first met her.

Her offer today had not been unexpected.

'I'm afraid,' I said, 'you've come to the wrong person. I must refuse.'

'I see,' Monica said.

'She's been working on her scowl,' J.C. said appreciatively from where he leaned against the wall. 'It's getting better.'

'If you would *look* at the camera . . .' Monica said.

'When I saw it last, it was in at least sixteen pieces,' I said. 'There's just not anything to work with.'

She narrowed her eyes at me. She still suspected I'd dropped it on purpose as the explosion hit. It didn't help that Razon's body had been burned to near unrecognizability in the subsequent explosions and fire that had consumed the building. Any items he'd had on him – secrets that explained how the camera *really* worked – had been destroyed.

'I'll admit,' I said, leaning forward, 'that I'm not terribly sorry to discover you can't fix the thing. I'm not certain the world is prepared for the information it could provide.' *Or, at least, I'm not certain the world is prepared for people like you controlling that information.*

'But—'

'Monica, I don't know what I could do that your engineers haven't. We're simply going to have to accept the fact that this technology died with Razon. If what he did was anything other than a hoax. To be honest, I'm increasingly certain it was one. Razon was tortured beyond what a simple scientist could have endured, yet did not give the terrorists what they wanted. It was because he couldn't. It was all a sham.'

She sighed and stood up. 'You are passing up on greatness, Mister Leeds.'

'My dear,' I said, standing, 'you should know by now that I've already *had* greatness. I traded it for mediocrity and some measure of sanity.'

'You should ask for a refund,' she said. 'Because I'm not certain I have found either in you.' She took something from her pocket and dropped it on the table. A large envelope.

'And this is?' I asked, taking it.

'We found film in the camera,' she said. 'Only one image was recoverable.'

I hesitated, then slipped the picture out. It was in black and white, like the others. It depicted a man, bearded and robed, sitting – though on what, I couldn't see. His face was striking. Not because of its shape, but because it was looking *directly* at the camera. A camera that wouldn't be there for two thousand years.

'We think it comes from the Triumphal Entry,' she said. 'The background, at least, looks to be the Beautiful Gate. It's hard to tell.'

'My God,' Ivy whispered, stepping up beside me.

Those eyes ... I stared at the photo. Those *eyes*.

'Hey, I thought we weren't supposed to swear around you,' J.C. called to Ivy.

'It wasn't a curse,' she said, resting her fingers reverently on the photo. 'It was an identification.'

'It's meaningless, unfortunately,' Monica said. 'There's no way to prove who that is. Even if we could, it wouldn't do anything toward proving or disproving Christianity. This was before the man was killed. Of all the shots for Razon to get ...' She shook her head.

'It doesn't change my mind,' I said, slipping the photo back into the envelope.

'I didn't think it would,' Monica said. 'Consider it as payment.'

'I didn't end up accomplishing much for you.'

'Nor we for you,' she said, walking from the room. 'Good evening, Mister Leeds.'

I rubbed my finger on the envelope, listening as Wilson showed Monica to the door, then shut it. I left Ivy and J.C. having a conversation about his cursing, then walked into the entryway and up the stairs. I wound around them, hand on the banister, before reaching the upper hallway.

My study was at the end. The room was lit by a single lamp on the desk, the shades drawn against the night. I walked to my desk and sat down. Tobias sat in one of the two other chairs beside it.

I picked up a book – the last in what had been a huge stack – and began leafing through. The picture of Sandra, the one recovered from the train station, hung tacked to the wall beside me.

'Have they figured it out?' Tobias asked.

'No,' I said. 'Have you?'

'It was never the camera, was it?'

I smiled, turning a page. 'I searched his pockets right after he died. Something cut my fingers. Broken glass.'

Tobias frowned. Then, after a moment's thought, he smiled. 'Shattered lightbulbs?'

I nodded. 'It wasn't the camera, it was the *flash*. When Razon took pictures at the church, he used the flash even outside in the sunlight. Even when his subject was well lit, even when he was trying to capture something that happened during the day, such as Jesus' appearance outside the tomb following his resurrection. That's a mistake a good photographer wouldn't make. And he was a good photographer, judging by the pictures hung in his apartment. He had a good eye for lighting.'

I turned a page, then reached into my pocket and took something out, setting it on the table. A detachable flash, the one I'd taken off the camera just before the explosion. 'I'm not sure if it's something about the flash mechanism or the bulbs, but I do know he was swapping out the bulbs in order to stop the thing from working when he didn't want it to.'

'Beautiful,' Tobias said.

'We'll see,' I replied. 'This flash doesn't work; I've tried. I don't know what's wrong with it. You know how the cameras would work for Monica's people for a while? Well, many camera flashes have multiple bulbs like this one. I suspect that only one of these had anything to do with the temporal effects. The special bulbs burned out quickly, after maybe ten shots.'

I turned a few pages.

'You're changing, Stephen,' Tobias finally said. 'You noticed this without Ivy. Without any of us. How long before you don't need us any longer?'

'I hope that never happens,' I said. 'I don't want to be that man.'

'And yet you chase *her*.'

'And yet I do,' I whispered.

One step closer. I knew what train Sandra had taken. A ticket peeked out of her coat pocket. I could make out the numbers, just barely.

She'd gone to New York. For ten years, I'd been hunting this answer – which was only a tiny fraction of a much larger hunt. The trail was a decade old, but it was *something*.

For the first time in years, I was making progress. I closed the book and sat back, looking up at Sandra's picture. She was beautiful. So very beautiful.

Something rustled in the dark room. Neither Tobias nor I stirred as a short, balding man sat down at the desk's empty chair. 'My name is Arnaud,' he said. 'I'm a physicist specializing in temporal mechanics, causality, and quantum theories. I believe you have a job for me?'

I set the final book on the stack of those I'd read during the last month. 'Yes, Arnaud,' I said. 'I do.'

ACKNOWLEDGMENTS

As always, my wonderful wife Emily gets a big thumbs-up for dealing with the sometimes erratic life of a professional writer. The incumbent Peter Ahlstrom did quite a bit of special work on this project. Another person of note is Moshe Feder, who gave me one of my very early reads on this book – and who discussed thoughts, possibilities, and conjectures regarding it from its earliest days.

My agent, Joshua Bilmes, has been his usual awesome self. Other early readers include Brian T. Hill, Dominique Nolan, Kaylynn ZoBell, Ben Olsen, Danielle Olsen, Karen Ahlstrom, Dan Wells, Alan Layton, and Ethan Skarstedt.

A special thanks to Subterranean Press for giving this work a place in print. Bill Schafer and Yanni Kuznia have been fantastic.

Brandon Sanderson